JUNGLEWALK

NANCY TAFURI

GREENWILLOW BOOKS · NEW YORK

IN MEMORY OF PAUL HIRSCHMAN

Watercolors, colored pencils,
and a black line were used for
the full-color illustrations.
The typeface is Windsor.
Copyright © 1988
by Nancy Tafuri

Greenwillow Books, a division of
William Morrow & Company, Inc.,
1350 Avenue of the Americas,
New York, NY 10019.
Printed in Hong Kong by
South China Printing Co.

First Edition
10 9 8 7 6 5 4 3

Library of Congress
Cataloging-in-Publication Data

Tafuri, Nancy.
Junglewalk.
Summary: A little boy falls asleep
after reading a book about animals
in a jungle, and then he meets
them all in his dream.
[1. Jungle animals—Fiction.
2. Dreams—Fiction.
3. Stories without words]
I. Title.   PZ7.T117Ju 1988
[E]   87-8558
ISBN 0-688-07182-1
ISBN 0-688-07183-X (lib. bdg.)